S. J. Charlie is a self-employed writer, hailing from the seaside town of South Shields. From her earliest days, she found solace and inspiration in crafting stories. After earning a degree from the Open University, S. J. Charlie embarked on a dedicated journey as a writer. Immersing herself in her craft, she spent countless hours honing her skills. It was in the realm of children's literature that S. J. Charlie discovered her true calling. She set out to make her mark as an author, weaving enchanting tales that captivate the hearts and minds of young readers.

# S. J. Charlie

# The Great HISSES HISS

**Austin Macauley Publishers**
LONDON * CAMBRIDGE * NEW YORK * SHARJAH

**Copyright © S. J. Charlie 2025**

The right of **S. J. Charlie** to be identified as authors of this work has been asserted by them in accordance with sections 77 and 78 of the Copyright, Designs and Patents Act 1988.

All rights reserved. No part of this publication may be reproduced, stored in a retrieval system, or transmitted in any form or by any means, electronic, mechanical, photocopying, recording, or otherwise, without the prior permission of the publishers.

Any person who commits any unauthorised act in relation to this publication may be liable to criminal prosecution and civil claims for damages.

A CIP catalogue record for this title is available from the British Library.

ISBN 9781035871858 (Paperback)
ISBN 9781035871865 (ePub e-book)

www.austinmacauley.com

First Published 2025
Austin Macauley Publishers Ltd®
1 Canada Square
Canary Wharf
London
E14 5AA

To my partner, who has been with me every step of the way, guiding me, supporting me, and believing in me. This book is dedicated to you, with all my gratitude and affection.

I extend my deepest gratitude to my partner, whose unwavering presence and unwavering support have been my rock throughout this journey. Your belief in me has fuelled my determination, and I am endlessly grateful for your love and encouragement.

I would also like to express my heartfelt thanks to Austin Macauley Publishers. Your incredible dedication and support throughout the publishing process have been invaluable. The professionalism and guidance provided by your team have made this endeavour truly remarkable. Thank you for believing in my work and for helping to bring my vision to life.

# Chapter One

On a sunny day in the enchanting dinosaur world, where rays of sunlight filtered through the towering shades of green trees, painting dappled patterns on the forest floor, a thrilling adventure was about to unfold. The great Hisses Hiss, a unique and colourful dinosaur, was on a quest to hunt his prey in the lush undergrowth. His striking blue-green and pink frills swayed gently as he moved, and his sharp grey and red face was locked onto his target – a single dodo, waddling through the forest.

Hisses Hiss's heart raced as he prepared to make his move.

But just as he was about to pounce, a sudden flash of feathers crossed his vision, and the dodo vanished from sight. Hisses Hiss turned his head, his frills still raised, to find a proud Raptor holding the dodo in its jaws. The familiar Raptor was larger and more menacing, with its yellow feathers atop his head, sharp teeth, and gleaming green scales. "Hey, Raptor!" Hisses Hiss called out, emerging from the undergrowth and approaching the Raptor.

The Raptor, with the dodo still in its jaws, turned to face him. "Can I help you, Hisses Hiss?" the Raptor mumbled, the dodo still causing a ruckus.

"That was my dinner! I was about to pounce before you interrupted," Hisses Hiss exclaimed, his disappointment clear. With a thud, the Raptor dropped the dodo to the ground, and the frightened bird scurried away, squawking loudly, visibly agitated by the unexpected

turn of events.

Raptor spoke, "Sorry, I didn't mean to. I thought you would be hunting with your father."

Hisses Hiss paused, his mind drifting back to an unpleasant memory from school that very day. A bully had taunted him, saying, "You are useless. You can't hunt without your papa. How pathetic!"

In response, Hisses Hiss had vowed, "I will show you. Just wait. I will become the best dinosaur around, the great Hisses Hiss.

Now, Hisses Hiss lifted his head and declared, "I am the great Hisses Hiss, the best dinosaur in all the lands. I don't need my papa," his voice tinged with frustration and sadness.

The Raptor raised an eyebrow and said, "The great Hisses Hiss, the best dinosaur in all the lands? That doesn't sound like you." He looked at Hisses Hiss with a puzzled expression, sensing that something was amiss. Unbeknownst to Hisses Hiss, the Raptor had recently had a conversation with Mr. Hiss, and it had led him on a journey to find Hisses Hiss and help him understand the true value of his uniqueness. Raptor recalls the conversation he engaged in with the father of the young dinosaur earlier that day.

"Raptor!" Mr. Hiss's urgent voice called out, and Raptor turned to see Mr. Hiss hurrying towards him, a worried expression on his grey and red face.

"Oh, hello, Mr. Hiss," Raptor greeted, noticing the deep concern etched on his friend's face. "You look quite worried," Raptor pointed out.

Mr. Hiss nodded solemnly. "Well, that's because I am," he admitted. His blue and green frills quivered nervously as he spoke. "It's Hisses Hiss. He decided to go out hunting alone today."

Raptor, who had always held a special fondness for the young Hisses Hiss, found himself taken aback. "This is unlike Hisses Hiss," he mused, reflecting on the dinosaur's usual routine, which primarily revolved around accompanying his father, Mr Hiss on their hunting expeditions.

This recent change was indeed peculiar. Raptor had shared a close bond with the Hiss family since Hisses Hiss was but a hatchling. Mr. Hiss continued with a worried tone, "Yes, I am quite afraid, but he was insistent about it. I think that he has been having problems at school. He always seems so upset about it, when he is finished school." Raptor nodded in understanding.

"I was wondering if you could help. If you see him, could you keep an eye on him for me?" Mr. Hiss asked, hope in his eyes.

"Of course, I would be happy to," Raptor replied with a warm smile, putting Mr. Hiss's concerns at ease. Mr. Hiss breathed a sigh of relief, feeling grateful for Raptor's support.

"Thank you, Raptor. You are a good friend. I saw him go towards the meadow.

Please keep an eye on him. And if you could try to investigate what is wrong with him, I would be most thankful," Mr. Hiss requested. Continuing, he shared, "In my youth, my father imparted a valuable lesson. He taught me that acknowledging the greatness in others, even when I felt at my best, was a source of strength. It guided me through

my younger days. Perhaps I could offer that perspective to young Hisses Hiss if you think it might help."

Mr. Hiss's face brightened with hope. "Oh, if you would be so kind, Raptor. I've tried to ask him, but he doesn't say anything. Maybe getting a new perspective will help," Mr. Hiss said, thankful for Raptor's support. Raptor snapped back to the present.

The young Hisses Hiss, determined to prove his worth, declared with pride, "I am the great Hisses Hiss, the best around. That's me."

With a playful grin that revealed all his sharp teeth, Raptor couldn't help but be amused. He inquired, "What makes you think you're the best, Hisses Hiss?"

Undaunted, Hisses Hiss responded confidently, "Well, look at me! I am brave and adventurous, without fear – the great Hisses Hiss!" His frills extended, and he hissed louder, emphasizing his point.

Raptor observed Hisses Hiss and couldn't help but smile. "You are quite the fierce one. You remind me of myself when I was young and thought I could take on the entire world," Raptor shared with a hearty laugh. Hisses Hiss was intrigued.

"What do you mean? I can take on the entire world! I am the great Hisses Hiss."

Recognizing an opportunity to impart a meaningful lesson, reminiscent of the wisdom his father had shared with him in his youth, Raptor suggested, "What if today, you and I embark on a joint hunting expedition? I'd love to demonstrate to the remarkable Hisses Hiss just how incredible and talented other dinosaurs can be.

"Eager to share the wisdom acquired over the years, Raptor

continued, "We can visit some of my friends, and I'll show you the awe-inspiring qualities of different dinosaurs. Your father won't mind; after all, we're best friends." Raptor concluded with a friendly grin.

Hisses Hiss hesitated but then relented, "Well, I guess the great Hisses Hiss could come with you for the day. You are a close friend of the family, but just to prove that Hisses Hiss is the great and best dinosaur."

"Great!" Raptor exclaimed with a smile.

With Hisses Hiss by his side, Raptor led him to a vast, grassy opening in the meadow. It was the perfect place to begin their adventure and discover the incredible talents of other dinosaurs. Hisses Hiss looked up at Raptor, and with a sense of excitement and determination, he declared, "So which dinosaur are we starting with? Who dares think they're better than the great Hisses Hiss?"

Raptor chuckled. "Well, we will start with me," he said, his pride evident as he grinned.

Hisses Hiss, determined to prove himself, couldn't help but let out a small, high-pitched laugh. "Well, I already know I am better than you," he playfully retorted to Raptor with a smile. "No offence, Raptor."

Raptor was prepared to showcase his unique skills. "Well, how about I show you what I can do first?" he suggested.

Hisses Hiss agreed, "I guess so."

"First, I am going to show you how quick and nimble a Raptor can be," Raptor said, his voice filled with confidence.

Hisses Hiss, ever eager to prove his worth, protested, "I can be

fast."

Raptor nodded and acknowledged Hisses Hiss's skills. "I know, young one. You are skilled in your unique style. But I am a Raptor, and I have different skills than you do. Watch," Raptor said as he stomped his feet on the ground beneath him before sprinting forward.

His heart raced, and his feet pounded the ground beneath him as he ran with lightning speed. The wind whipped his feathers back from his face, and he quickened his pace, culminating with a powerful leap that landed him gracefully on a high rock. "See, I am fast, I chase my prey, and I leap when the time is right. That's what Raptors do, young one," Raptor explained, his pride evident.

Hisses Hiss listened attentively, but as he approached Raptor, a shadow of doubt crossed his face.

"I am rapid, swift, and pounce on my prey with a sudden attack," Raptor continued.

"Whereas you stalk your prey, being silent and leaping when you are close enough to do the final strike," Raptor concluded with a warm smile.

Hisses Hiss couldn't help but recall the hurtful words of the bullies at school, who had mocked him for his unique approach. "Look how slow he is. Any dinosaur is better than him," they had taunted. Doubt began to fill Hisses Hiss's thoughts as he looked at Raptor.

But little did Hisses Hiss know that today's adventure was not just about showcasing skills. Each dinosaur possesses its unique strengths and qualities, making each one special in its particular remarkable way. Raptor, still smiling warmly, was ready to share this wisdom

with his young friend. Hisses Hiss, undeterred by Raptor's impressive display, was determined to prove himself. "Yeah, well, I could be fast. Just you watch," he declared with unwavering confidence.

Hisses Hiss hopped up and down for a moment, mustering all his energy, before dashing forward, convinced he was moving at lightning speed. In reality, Raptor watched with a patient smile as Hisses Hiss raced at his top speed, which, in truth, was not very fast at all. The Raptor could easily keep up by walking.

Suddenly, Hisses Hiss leapt and landed on a not-so-high rock, his face beaming with pride. "See, I am just as fast!" Hisses Hiss declared, feeling a surge of accomplishment.

But before Raptor could respond, Hisses Hiss cut him off, asserting, "Silence! Your point has failed. Hisses Hiss is better than Raptor."

Raptor knew that he had to help Hisses Hiss understand the value of each dinosaur's unique skills. "The great Hisses Hiss is the best dinosaur," Hisses Hiss cheered, extending his frills and hissing proudly. But Hisses Hiss appreciated Raptor's affection and said, "But you were good too, Raptor."

With a warm smile, Raptor spoke, "Thank you, Hisses Hiss, but I am not done yet.

We are going to go see my friend Rex the T-Rex.

I'll show you how amazing other dinosaurs can be, but not just by showing you myself." Hisses Hiss eagerly agreed,

"All right!" With Hisses Hiss in tow, Raptor led the way, ready to introduce his young friend to the incredible talents and qualities of their fellow dinosaurs. Raptor planned to visit Rex the T-Rex, who

was also a good friend of Mr. Hiss, who would help Hisses Hiss see the world from a new perspective.

"Come along then," Raptor urged with a cheerful smile, and together they ventured off to meet Rex the T-Rex. Hisses Hiss couldn't help but feel a sense of amazement at Raptor's incredible speed. He watched as Raptor moved so swiftly that Hisses Hiss could barely keep up with his eyes. But even amid this excitement, a cloud of self-doubt loomed over him. "You are the worst dinosaur I have ever seen!" The hurtful words of the little dinosaurs at school echoed in Hisses Hiss's mind, causing his cheerful demeanour to fade. Raptor noticed the sadness on Hisses Hiss's face and sensed that something was deeply troubling the young dinosaur.

Raptor, having experienced similar feelings of doubt and sadness when he was young, was determined to help Hisses Hiss. "Is everything all right, Hisses Hiss?" Raptor gently inquired, his concern evident.

Hisses Hiss hesitated but quickly replied, "Fine, perfectly fine." He put on a brave face, just as Raptor used to do when he was little. When he didn't want to burden anyone with his worries. Raptor wasn't convinced by the swift response. He was aware that at times, the gentle guidance of a caring friend could be the catalyst needed for someone to share their thoughts and feelings.

"Are you sure?" Raptor asked, giving Hisses Hiss a reassuring look.

Hisses Hiss hesitated, "Yes," he replied, still holding back the deeper concerns that weighed on his heart. But there was a glimmer of hope in Hisses Hiss's eyes.

Raptor knew that Hisses Hiss needed more than just a display of

skills; he needed someone to talk to and understand his feelings. "Come on, then, Hiss," Raptor said with a warm and encouraging smile, inviting Hisses Hiss to join him in the journey ahead. Hisses Hiss looked up at Raptor, and despite the lingering worries, he seemed a little happier, that he wasn't alone on this adventure.

# Chapter Two

Amidst the tall grasses and towering oak trees, Raptor and Hisses Hiss embarked on their adventure, their footsteps weaving a path through the forest floor. Leaves descended with a poetic grace, weaving a mesmerizing mosaic of dappled sunlight.

They painted the earth with vibrant hues as they journeyed toward their destination, none other than the legendary Rex—a colossal and majestic T-Rex renowned far and wide. As they walked, the mighty Rex came into view. He was so colossal that he dwarfed even the tallest trees, and Hisses Hiss, who was much smaller in comparison, couldn't help but be taken aback by Rex's sheer size.

Rex's scales were a combination of brown and black, and his formidable teeth gleamed menacingly. He was scanning the surroundings, his head swaying from side to side as he searched for something to eat. "Hello, Rex! It's Raptor and young Hisses Hiss!" Raptor called out in a voice that would reach Rex. The T-Rex turned his colossal head and, upon seeing Hisses Hiss with Raptor, broke into a welcoming smile, his sharp teeth revealed. "Well, hello, Raptor. Nice to see you. Hello, little one.

It's odd to see you without your father," Rex greeted with a rumbling voice.

Hisses Hiss couldn't resist the opportunity to assert his newfound identity. "Well, I don't need my father. I am the great Hisses Hiss, the most skilled and best dinosaur in the lands," he proudly declared,

extending his frills and hissing for emphasis.

Rex's deep laughter rumbled through the air. "Well, how are you the best dinosaur? Don't you think all of us are extraordinary and unique?" Rex mused, his wise eyes filled with kindness.

"That's what I have been trying to teach him—how we are all different," Raptor chimed in, as he leaned close to Rex and whispered in a low voice, "Between you and me, something is wrong with Hisses Hiss."

Rex, who had keenly observed Hisses Hiss's unusual behaviour, raised an inquisitive brow. He knew that if Raptor was concerned, there must be a reason. He offered a reassuring smile in response.

"Well, how about I show you what a T-Rex can do, little one?" Rex proposed to Hisses Hiss, eager to help. Hisses Hiss, intrigued by the prospect, replied,

"I guess that the great Hisses Hiss could take some time to see what you can do, Rex." Rex beamed with delight.

"Splendid!" he exclaimed with a grin, while Raptor joined in the excitement.

"Now, little one, a T-Rex is different from Raptors and Dilophosaurus like yourself," Rex began to explain, but Hisses Hiss interrupted,

"You mean Hisses Hiss like me."

Both Rex and Raptor exchanged a puzzled look before turning their gaze back to Hisses Hiss. Raptor gently corrected him, "You do know that you are a Dilophosaurus, Hiss."

Hisses Hiss, seemingly baffled, maintained his position. "No, I am a Hisses Hiss," he stated with an innocent expression, unknowingly causing his friends to share a knowing smile. Rex, slightly disgruntled but still eager to teach, continued, "Fine then, Hisses Hiss, like yourself. A T-Rex is big and noisy, but we are fierce as well as courageous."

Capturing Hisses Hiss's attention, Rex directed his head towards a substantial log nestled in the verdant grass. "Do you see that log over there?"

Hisses Hiss nodded, intrigued by the question. "Yes, I do." However, upon closer examination, Hisses Hiss realized that what appeared as a log from Rex's viewpoint was, in fact, a tree.

With an innocent earnestness, he couldn't resist the urge to kindly correct Rex, saying, "Actually, Rex, that's a tree, not a log." Rex couldn't help but laugh heartily.

"Well, pretend it's a fierce creature and watch how I approach it," he suggested.

Rex, despite his enormous size, began to run surprisingly fast for a T-Rex. His pace quickened, and he let out a thunderous roar that displayed all his menacing teeth—a roar capable of striking fear into the heart of any dinosaur. The ground rumbled and shook with the terrifying sound, leaving Hisses Hiss and Raptor in awe of Rex's fierceness.

Rex then picked up the so-called 'log' with his massive teeth, making it seem as light as a twig. His sharp teeth effortlessly snapped through the wood as he shook the log and slammed it onto the ground with his mighty talons, piercing the wood.

He roared once more and crunched a piece of the log with his powerful jaw and teeth. Finally, Rex snapped the rest of the log and

let it fall to the ground in pieces.

With the task completed, Rex walked over proudly to where Raptor and Hisses Hiss stood. Raptor and Hisses Hiss now felt quite small in comparison to the massive T-Rex. "Wow, Rex, that was amazing. You are so large and fierce; you could take on anything," Raptor praised, a genuine smile on his face.

"Well, that's because I am a T-Rex. I am huge and strong," Rex replied. He then turned his attention to Hisses Hiss, recognizing that the young dinosaur was dealing with some inner doubts. "But you, Hisses Hiss, could sneak by me, and I would never have noticed you."

As the echoes of past taunts from bullies resurfaced in Hisses Hiss's mind, "You are so weak; you will never be strong like me," the bullies had sneered.

"Yeah, well, I am strong too," Hisses Hiss declared with newfound determination, making both Raptor and Rex look at him with a mixture of curiosity and surprise.

"I bet you could be, Hisses Hiss, but…" Rex tried to explain before being cut off by Hisses Hiss's resolute cry, "Silence! The great Hisses Hiss can do this."

Hisses Hiss then walked over to a substantial stick on the ground. His determination was fuelled by the doubts cast upon him by his fellow dinosaurs at school, who had labelled him weak.

Unbeknownst to him, he was unaware of the lesson Rex and Raptor were trying to impart. "Well, I can see that something is wrong with the little guy," Rex noted, his gaze filled with understanding. Raptor, too, recognized that Hisses Hiss needed more than just physical

demonstrations of strength. He required an appreciation for the significance of each dinosaur's distinct qualities, a lesson both Raptor and Rex were resolute in imparting to him.

"He's young, thinks he can take on the world," Raptor replied, his fondness for Hisses Hiss evident.

Rex chuckled and turned to Raptor saying, "Reminds me of you when you were young," with a grin that made Raptor chuckle and beam.

"But it's not just that," Raptor continued, growing more serious. "Hisses Hiss has never been like this. He loves his father, and the fact that he came out today without him is not like him," Raptor expressed his worry.

"I agree. I've never seen him without his father. He was always happy with him. I wonder why he wants to prove himself," Rex mused. "Hisses Hiss is kind and listens to others."

"Trouble is afoot. Mr Hiss entrusted me with the task of watching over him today, expressing deep concern for his well-being. I vowed to impart the wisdom passed down from my father, but alas, my attempts at guidance appear to be falling short," Raptor conceded.

"I remember that day. Your father came to mine, didn't he?" Rex asked, and Raptor nodded.

"You were like Hisses Hiss—didn't listen. Maybe we need someone with more experience," Rex said thoughtfully. "While my father possessed wisdom, I daresay neither of us has amassed enough wisdom as of yet."

As they discussed Hisses Hiss's situation, Hisses Hiss himself was

persistently trying to break the large stick.

He extended his frills, hissed at it loudly, and shook it vigorously, attempting to snap it in his teeth. Rex and Raptor watched his tenacious struggle, and Rex couldn't help but chuckle.

"I love how stubborn he is," Rex said with a laugh.

Raptor added, "He gets that from his father," and they both shared a hearty laugh.

Finally, with determination, Hisses Hiss slammed the stick on the ground, visibly frustrated that it hadn't broken yet. He extended his frills and hissed once more, this time placing his foot on the stick, which finally caused it to snap. Pleased with his accomplishment, Hisses Hiss walked back to where Raptor and Rex stood.

"Here we go again. How are we going to understand what's wrong with him?"

Raptor expressed his concern. "He doesn't want to talk about it. What do we do?" he asked.

"I have an idea," Rex said to Raptor, who looked at him curiously. "As you see, the great Hisses Hiss has proved himself to be just as strong as a T-Rex."

Hisses Hiss proudly cried out, "I am the best dinosaur in the land!" and Raptor let out a sigh, wondering how they could get through to their young friend and uncover the source of his inner turmoil.

Rex continued to watch Hisses Hiss's behaviour, sensing that there was more to the story than the young dinosaur was willing to reveal. "Is there anything wrong, Hisses Hiss?" he asked, a note of concern in his deep voice.

"No, I am fine," Hisses Hiss protested, but the doubt in his eyes was evident.

Rex and Raptor shared a knowing look before Rex proposed, "What if we paid a visit to my venerable friend, the Elder Brachiosaurus? Perhaps Hisses Hiss could benefit from the wisdom of age."

Rex exchanged a glance with Raptor before suggesting, "Hisses Hiss, can we all go see my friend, the Elder, he is a Brachiosaurus?"

Raptor chimed in, "Yeah, Hisses Hiss, how about it? the Elder is meant to be very wise." Hisses Hiss reflected on the regular visits his Papa and Raptor made to seek guidance from the Brachiosaurus. He also recalled his papa finding genuine enjoyment in the company of the wise Elder.

Perhaps, in his endeavours to prove his worth to others, Hisses Hiss was inadvertently seeking validation within himself. Yet, Rex was powerful and huge, and his father, Mr. Hiss, often visited the Brachiosaurus for wisdom. "All right," Hisses Hiss agreed proudly, his heart warming at the thought of spending time with his friends and the wise Elder.

"Great, then let's get going," Rex said with a grin, as they set off together on a journey to see the wise Brachiosaurus, hoping that the Elder might have some answers for their young friend.

# Chapter Three

Down by the riverside, Rex, Raptor, and Hisses Hiss made their way, the towering Brachiosaurus standing out amidst the greenery. The massive Brachiosaurus was easily distinguishable as the largest dinosaur around. "Elder," Rex called to the Brachiosaurus, who was busy munching on the leaves of a tall tree. The ancient dinosaur turned his head upon hearing his name, and his kind eyes peered down at the trio.

"Greetings," the Elder said, his voice rumbling in a low, gentle tone. He bent his long neck down, so he was at eye level with them. "Well, hello! You all look as if you are on an adventure," he remarked with a warm smile.

"Hello, Elder. It's nice to see you again," Raptor replied, grinning.

"Indeed," the Elder replied with a smile. "You too, Raptor."

Rex then addressed the wise Elder, saying, "Hello, old friend. Both Raptor and I could use your help." He gestured toward Hisses Hiss.

"This is Hisses Hiss."

The Elder looked down at Hisses Hiss.

"The great Hisses Hiss Rex," Hisses Hiss said beaming with pride.

"I have seen you around with your father, but today, you look troubled," the Elder observed.

Hisses Hiss responded defiantly, "I don't need my father. I am the best dinosaur in the land." The Elder's laughter echoed through the landscape, a deep and rumbling sound that hinted at the weight of

countless ages.

His eyes, filled with wisdom earned over time, studied Hisses Hiss with a mixture of amusement and understanding. The young dinosaur's proclamation had sparked a recognition in the Elder's ancient mind, a recognition born from witnessing the struggles and growth of many like Hisses Hiss. With a knowing smile, the Elder spoke in a voice that carried the echoes of countless stories. "Ah, young one, your hisses may be fierce, but they are not unfamiliar to these ancient ears."

"Now, why do you think that? Don't you think we are all individuals and unique?" he asked the young Dilophosaurus.

Hisses Hiss struggled to find the right words. "Well," he began, "I…"

The Elder shared a valuable insight with Hisses Hiss. "I've met many dinosaurs similar to yourself. Raptor here used to be the same when he was young, saying he could take on the whole world," the Elder said, and Raptor smiled and laughed in acknowledgement.

Raptor then explained, "My father showed me one day, just like I'm doing with you Hisses Hiss, he showed me that each of us holds significance in our unique ways.

Hisses Hiss looked at Raptor, his curiosity piqued. "Well, I did everything that Raptor and Rex did," he asserted. Raptor and Rex exchanged doubtful glances, prompting the Elder to intervene.

"How about I show you what I can do, Hisses Hiss, if you have the time?" he proposed politely.

"I guess so," Hisses Hiss replied.

"Great," the Elder said with a smile, winking at Raptor and Rex as

they hatched a plan. The Brachiosaurus then ascended to its majestic height, its head soaring into the heavens.

"See, Hisses Hiss, in comparison, you are the smallest dinosaur here," Raptor pointed out.

Hisses Hiss, ever defiant, retorted, "Yeah, well, I could beat you and Rex in a second."

Rex clarified the Elder's message, saying, "That's not what he is trying to say, Hisses Hiss. What Raptor is saying is that, whether small or big, thin or giant like myself, we are all different." The Elder leaned his head down and smiled as he continued, "Well, first, I am tall. So tall that I can reach the top of trees." With ease, he reached up to a tree's top branches, plucking them off and placing them on the ground. The branch he held in his mouth was larger than Hisses Hiss.

"Wow, Elder, you are so tall. I couldn't imagine what it would be like to be as tall as the trees. You can almost touch the clouds," Raptor said with admiration.

The elder laughed heartily. "Well, thank you, Raptor. That's very kind of you. Rex and I have our advantages to being this big."

Rex chimed in, "Yes, Elder is right, but being small has its advantages too. You and Raptor can be fast, hidden, and also stalk your prey and pounce on them," Rex explained, highlighting the unique strengths of every dinosaur.

Rex spoke gently, "I and Brachiosaurus are big, but we can't hide or pounce, yet we are tall and strong."

Raptor added, "See, Hisses Hiss, we're all different," smiling warmly.

Hisses Hiss nodded in agreement but then lowered his head and admitted, "Yes, I understand that, but I have to be better than I am."

This seized the attention of Raptor Rex and the Elder, drawing their focus to the young dinosaur "Hisses Hiss, what do you mean by that?" Raptor inquired, a concerned look on his face.

The Elder, with his wisdom, also wanted to know more. "Hisses Hiss, what has happened to make you think this way?" he asked gently.

Hisses Hiss let out a sigh and confessed, "I've been keeping this to myself, but at school, a clique of dinosaurs has been hurling unkind and hurtful words at me. Saying I am weak and small," he confessed.

Continuing, he shared, "It's been distressing, and after today's incident, it became overwhelming. I wanted to prove, to demonstrate to them and perhaps to myself that I am superior, the best dinosaur in these lands. That's why I venture out alone today. That's why I wanted to be the great Hisses Hiss."

Rex expressed concern and asked, "Hisses Hiss, that is bullying. Have you not told your parents or teachers?"

Hisses Hiss admitted, "No, I haven't. I didn't want to look weak by asking for help."

The Elder spoke reassuringly, "Hisses Hiss, asking for help is never a weakness. Don't think that."

Raptor asked, "Do all the dinosaurs at school do this?"

Hisses Hiss replied, "No, many of the dinosaurs are quite friendly. However, that doesn't make it any less challenging. The four dinosaurs single me out for bullying, and only me."

The Elder offered words of wisdom, "Young one, it is very easy to

doubt yourself in life, but that doesn't mean you should be alone. You have friends and family that care about you."

Raptor chimed in, "Elder is right, Hisses Hiss. Your father sent me to look for you today; he was worried about you."

Hisses Hiss was surprised and asked, "He did?"

Raptor confirmed, "Yes, he did."

Hisses Hiss smiled and shared, "I didn't want to look weak by hunting with my Papa, but I love hunting with him. Mama says I am his little shadow."

Raptor offered comforting words, "You really should have opened up to your father, Hisses Hiss. Embracing moments with family is never a sign of weakness; instead, it's an opportunity to cherish the bonds that matter most."

Rex added, "Yes we always see you with him," smiling kindly.

Brachiosaurus smiled kindly as well and said, "Such a nice thing to see you and your father out together."

Hisses Hiss admitted, "I love going out with my Papa. It's just that after what the dinosaurs said, I doubted myself and thought I needed to do it without him."

Raptor spoke with heartfelt reassurance, "Hisses Hiss, both your parents and friends cherish you deeply. You are a kind and gentle natural soul, and you need to remember you're never alone. You have love and care surrounding you, disregard what the dinosaurs said; their words don't define the truth of who you are."

The Elder, his wisdom resonating in each word, gently spoke, "Hisses Hiss, allow me to share a profound truth with you. In this

vast world, each of us—yourself, me, Rex, and Raptor—possesses a unique essence, a special quality that sets us apart. You, my dear friend, are the only Hisses Hiss in the entire world, and that makes you extraordinarily special."

Hisses Hiss acknowledged, "I've truly enjoyed today, and I thought I had to face the bullies alone."

Raptor reassured him, "You're never on your own, Hisses Hiss."

Hisses Hiss came to a realization, "I should have seen that, I doubted myself and kept it to myself, Now I understand I should have confided in someone."

Encouragingly, Raptor added, "You shouldn't carry everything alone, Hisses Hiss."

Hisses Hiss admitted, "I always tell my papa everything, but I was so worried that he would think I was helpless."

Raptor assured him, "He would never think that."

Hisses Hiss realized, "I understand that now. I shouldn't have been scared. I should have told someone." With newfound determination, Hisses Hiss declared, "I need to talk to my mom and dad about this and apologize. I never intended to hurt or cause worry for my papa."

Rex smiled and said, "Yes, Hisses Hiss, you should tell your papa." Hisses Hiss, Raptor, Rex, and the Elder shared smiles and laughter. Hisses Hiss had come to understand the importance of seeking help and sharing his feelings with his loved ones. With renewed confidence and a sense of self-worth, he was eager to share his experiences with his papa and mama.

"I got to tell my mom and dad," Hisses Hiss exclaimed. The wise

Elder Raptor and the friendly Rex chuckled.

"Would you all come with me?" he asked.

"Of course, Hiss!" Rex replied, and the others nodded. As they headed back toward Hisses Hiss's home, they knew they had shared a special day. Hisses Hiss had made new friends and learned valuable life lessons, and how vital it is to stick together and celebrate what makes us all special.

They walked home together with a sense of unity and friendship. Hisses Hiss now knows that he can always rely on his friends for support and understanding and so, the day ended with the promise of better days ahead for Hisses Hiss, who had discovered the strength in sharing his feelings and leaning on his friends and family. The promise of more awesome days lay ahead, thanks to the power of friendship!